Classics For Kids

Sherlock Holmes
The Blue Carbuncle

re-told for children by

Mark Williams

Odyssey

ISBN: 978-1540497529

How old were you

when you

discovered Sherlock?

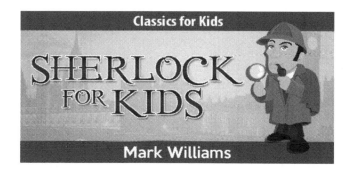

Sherlock For Kids on Facebook

Titles in this series include:

The Blue Carbuncle
Silver Blaze
The Red-Headed League
The Engineer's Thumb
The Speckled Band
The Six Napoleons
The Naval Treaty

Coming soon:

The Musgrave Ritual
The Beryl Coronet
The Gold Pince-Nez

The Blue Carbuncle 1

London, England. 1889.

IT WAS BOXING DAY, the day after Christmas Day, as I made my way carefully through the icy London streets. A cold wind blew light, fluffy snowflakes about and I hoped it wouldn't snow too heavily that afternoon.

The streets were icy and slippery and I found it easier to walk on the straw strewn across the road than on the pavements. By the time I got to my destination I was absolutely freezing. It was high time I bought myself a new coat and gloves!

I stomped my boots on the first of the stone steps outside 221b Baker Street, so I would not traipse ice and grit into Mrs. Hudson's hallway. It had been some time since I had lived here, sharing an apartment with my dear friend Mr. Sherlock Holmes, and I still had a key, so I unlocked the door and let myself in.

"Mrs. Hudson!" I shouted through to the kitchen where I knew the lady of the house would be busy. Partly as a courtesy to let her know I was here; more in the hope she would see me shivering and offer a warm pot of tea.

Which of course she did, bless her.

"Merry Christmas, Dr. Watson," Mrs. Hudson said as she came into the hallway, wiping floury hands on her flowery apron. "My, you look quite frozen. Hurry yourself along up to Mr. Holmes this instant and I shall bring you both a pot of steaming hot tea."

"That would be most welcome, Mrs. Hudson," I said.

"And just look at my floury hands," the landlady went on. "Why, Dr. Watson, you must surely have known I was making your favourite scones today. The first batch will be coming out of the oven in no time."

"Splendid, Mrs. Hudson," I said. "Splendid. And with a pat of fresh butter and your wonderful home-made strawberry jam, of course."

"Of course," chuckled Mrs. Hudson.

I leaned in to Mrs. Hudson and whispered, "Don't tell anyone I said so, Mrs. H., but between the two of us you make far better scones than my dear wife, bless her."

"Oh, get away with you, Dr. Watson," Mrs. Hudson blushed, and she shuffled back into the kitchen, chuckling to herself.

I made my way up the stairs to the floor occupied

by my dear friend, and knocked once.

"Come in, Watson," Holmes called out.

The Blue Carbuncle 2.

I PUSHED OPEN THE door and the warmth from the blazing fire met me. I put my hat on the hat-stand just inside the door and began taking off my gloves, scarf and overcoat.

"And just how did you know it was me, Holmes?" I asked. "The way I walked up the stairs, perhaps? Or the way I shuffled along the landing?"

Holmes dismissed my question with a wave of his hand.

"Really, Watson," he said, "it did not need any special detective skills to know of *your* arrival. First off, the bell did not ring, so clearly the visitor had a key. The upstairs rooms are empty right now, which means only three people are privileged to have a key to this house. Mrs. Hudson and I, of course, and your good self."

I glanced across at my friend. "You said, *first off,* Holmes. So there's something else, I take it?"

"Secondly," continued Holmes, "you called out to

Mrs. Hudson while in the hallway, in that booming voice of yours. A discussion about scones and strawberry jam, if I am not mistaken."

I smiled as I put my coat on the peg and walked across to warm my hands in front of the burning coals. It was always so obvious when Holmes explained his logic.

My friend Sherlock Holmes was laid out on the sofa, feet up, wearing his favourite purple dressing gown. As a rule Holmes only got dressed if he was going out or if he was expecting visitors. He had been smoking his pipe, and reading the morning's newspapers, which were now crumpled on the floor.

But what immediately caught my eye were the magnifying glass and the forceps on a wooden chair stood next to the sofa, and, hanging from the back of the same wooden chair, a battered old hat.

I knew immediately this hat did not belong to Holmes, but the magnifying glass and forceps did, and they told me the hat must be a clue in some new case Holmes was working on.

"I see you are busy, Holmes," I said, as I made myself comfortable by the fire. "A Christmas mystery to solve?"

"It is nothing special," Holmes said. "Just a lost hat handed in to me by Peterson, the Commissionaire, along with a lost goose."

I stared at Holmes in surprise. "A goose, did you say?"

Holmes smiled. "A big, fat Christmas goose,

Watson. Some poor soul went home without his hat and without his Christmas goose, and late on Christmas Eve, of all days. I would imagine the poor man's wife was not best pleased yesterday when they had their Christmas dinner with no goose on the table."

"A missing hat and a missing goose?" I looked around the room. "I see the hat, Holmes," I said. "But not the goose."

"That is because it is even now roasting in Mrs. Peterson's oven," Holmes said.

"Mrs. Peterson's oven?" I stared in amazement at Holmes. "But what if the rightful owner returns to claim it?"

"More importantly, Watson, what if he does not?" said Holmes. "Another day and the goose would be of no use to anyone. Better that Peterson and his family enjoy it than it goes to waste, given Peterson was the one who found it."

"That's true enough," I said. "But Holmes, how on earth does one lose one's hat and one's Christmas goose at the same time? I mean, to lose one or the other is surely carelessness. But to lose both?"

The Blue Carbuncle 3.

"IT HAPPENED LIKE THIS, Watson," Holmes said, sucking on his pipe. "Peterson had been out late on Christmas Eve, and on his way home saw a scuffle between an elderly man and some youths. The man had been wearing this very hat, and was carrying a Christmas goose over his shoulder."

"So what happened then?" I asked.

Holmes stretched out on the sofa. "It seems the youths were a little lively, perhaps having had a few too many drinks for Christmas, and knocked the man's hat off. He in turn put his goose down and angrily waved his walking stick at the lads to warn them off. Unfortunately he was closer to a shop window than he realized, and accidentally thrust the walking stick through the glass."

"Goodness gracious," I said.

"At this point Peterson called out for them to be careful," Holmes went on. "But it seems that, when the crowd turned and saw Peterson, still in his

Commissionaire's uniform, they must have mistaken him for a policeman, for they all ran off."

"Including the man who broke the window, I presume," I said.

"Including the man who broke the window," Holmes confirmed. "Most probably he too thought that Peterson was a policeman. By the time Peterson got to the scene all that was left was this battered old hat and a fine Christmas goose."

"And earlier today you had been examining the hat for clues when I arrived," I said.

"Indeed so, Watson," Holmes said. "We have a name, but no address. The hat and goose belong to one Mr. Henry Baker. That was easily found out, because the goose had a card tied to its leg, with the wording *For Mrs. Henry Baker* on it. Also, the hat has the initials *H.B.* on the lining. But that's not very helpful. There will of course be hundreds of gentlemen by the name of Henry Baker here in big city like London. Far too many to try track down."

At this point there was a knock at the door and Mrs. Hudson entered with the promised pot of tea and buttered scones with jam.

"Here you are, gentlemen," she said, placing the tray on the table.

The teapot was covered with a special Christmas tea-cozy she had knitted. Along with the milk jug, sugar bowl, cups, saucers and teaspoons there was a plate piled high with buttered scones with strawberry jam.

"Mrs. Hudson. You are simply wonderful," I said. "And the buttered scones are wonderful too, And so is this splendid tea-cozy. Isn't that so, Holmes?"

But Holmes did not hear me, and seemed not to notice Mrs. Hudson or the tray of tea and scones, for he had picked up the battered hat again and was studying it carefully through the magnifying glass.

Mrs. Hudson gave me a knowing smile. She knew all about Holmes and his strange ways.

"Enjoy the scones, Dr. Watson," she said. "And do try to save at least one for Mr. Holmes for when he finally realises they are there."

The Blue Carbuncle 4.

"A HAT IS A HAT, HOLMES, surely," I said, biting into one of Mrs. Hudson's delicious scones as soon as the landlady had closed the door behind her. "Beyond the initials, *HB*, surely there is nothing more you can tell from examining that old thing?"

"You are right, Watson," Holmes said. "There is nothing whatsoever I can deduce from this old hat. Except that Mr. Baker is quite clever, and not so long ago earned a good wage."

I stopped chomping on my scone and looked at Holmes.

"And that lately," Holmes continued, "Mr. Baker has fallen on hard times and has taken to drinking to take his mind off his problems. Which may be why his wife no longer loves him as much as she once did."

I stared in astonishment at Holmes. "You can tell all that from an old hat?"

Holmes held out the hat and magnifying glass for

me to take. "Look for yourself," he said. "It is all there."

I took the hat and examined it carefully. It was an old black bowler hat that had seen better days. The red silk lining inside was faded, but the initials H.B. could clearly be seen. There was a crack in the hard bowl, and the whole thing was dusty, with faded spots that had been coloured black with writing ink.

I looked through the magnifying glass, but all this did was make larger what I had already seen. I look up at Holmes in bewilderment. "But there is nothing to see," I declared.

"Nothing?" asked Holmes. "But surely you can see the man is late middle-aged, with gray hair, recently cut, who does little exercise and has no gas in his house."

I handed the hat and magnifying glass back to Holmes. "Now you are surely joking," I said.

At this Holmes laughed out loud and, spying the pot of tea, poured himself a cup before turning to me to explain. And of course when he did explain it, it was all so obvious.

First Holmes popped the hat on his own head, and it fell down over his eyes, for it was several sizes too big. He pulled it off again and beamed at me. "Mr. Baker has a head much larger than mine," he said. "It surely must have a larger brain in it, so he must be clever."

"Maybe so," I said, "but what about the rest of it? His wife no longer loves him because he has fallen on hard times and drinks too much? That he is middle-aged with gray hair, recently cut, and has no gas in his house? That is just guess-work, surely?"

"On the contrary," said Holmes. "It is all here. You saw it with your own eyes."

"I did no such thing," I said.

"You saw everything I saw," Holmes said. "But, Watson, you did not try to make sense of what you saw."

I took another scone from the plate. "Then tell me, Holmes," I said, "how does this hat reveal all this information to you, but not to me."

The Blue Carbuncle 5.

"ELEMENTARY, MY DEAR Watson," Holmes said. "The hat is three years old, for this design became fashionable at that time. The lining is silk, not some cheaper fabric, and would have cost quite a lot when new. Clearly the hat is now old and needs replacing, but our Mr. Baker still wears it. Therefore three years ago Mr. Baker was in a better job than he is now."

"Confound it, Holmes, it is always so obvious once you explain it," I said. "But what about the rest? The recent haircut, and his not being one to exercise?"

"The silk lining has traces of hair-cream," Holmes said. "And in that cream are short gray hairs, just cut. There are recent sweat stains, and that tells me Mr. Baker is not used to exercise, for no-one would sweat normally at this time of year."

"Be that as it may," I said, wishing I had noticed all this myself, "but there is no way, Holmes, absolutely no way, you can tell from that hat that his wife no longer loves him, or that he has no gas in his house.

That is beyond even your powers, surely."

"There is nothing to it," said Holmes. "The hat is dusty, as you can plainly see, and the dust is house-dust. You can tell by looking through the magnifying glass. It seems like the hat has not been dusted for many weeks. Now tell me, dear Watson, would your wife let *you* go out in public in such a disgraceful fashion?"

"Of course not," I said. "Why, I cannot leave the house at all without Mrs. Watson finding something on me that needs brushing or cleaning or adjusting. Sometimes it takes me ten minutes to get out of the front door!"

"Because she loves you so," Holmes beamed. "But no less clearly Mrs. Baker does not lavish such attention on her own husband anymore."

"Or perhaps he has no wife," I said, pleased with myself for finding a weakness in my friend's theory. "Perhaps Mr. Baker is not married, or something happened that they no longer live together."

"You are forgetting the card tied to the leg of the goose, Watson," came the reply. *"For Mrs. Henry Baker."*

I sighed. Holmes had an answer for everything."Ah, but what about the gas?" I demanded.

"Candle wax," said Holmes matter-of-factly. "There are no less than five candle wax stains on the hat. One, or even two, might come from outside the home, but five? That surely tells us he has no gaslighting and carries candles frequently."

Before I could answer Holmes, the outside bell jangled loudly, followed by a fist pounding on the front door.

A smile spread across my friend's face. "Unless I am very much mistaken there is someone at the door for me."

"You are expecting visitors?"

"I am expecting no-one," said Holmes, as the bell jangled again, and the hammering at the door continued. "But anyone visiting Mrs. Hudson would know better than to tug on the bell like that, and the urgency of those pounding fists can only mean someone in need of my services."

We heard the front door open, but Mrs. Hudson's words were cut short as the man – for it was a man's voice – shouted "Mr. Holmes! Mr. Holmes!" in breathless tones and we heard him rush past Mrs. Hudson and storm up the stairs.

The Blue Carbuncle 6.

IT SOUNDED LIKE A herd of elephants charging up the staircase, and I could just imagine Mrs. Hudson looking on in amazement at this desperate visitor stomping a trail of ice and snow up the stairs.

Then the door to Holmes's apartment burst open and Peterson the Commissionaire raced into the room and stopped, breathless, before Holmes, who was still sat comfortably on the sofa.

"The goose, Mr. Holmes!" shouted Peterson excitedly. "The goose!"

Holmes and I stared at Peterson.

"What, has the goose somehow come alive in the oven and flown off through the window with your carrots in its beak?" asked Holmes. "Calm yourself, Peterson. Take a seat and tell me what has happened."

But instead of taking a seat, Peterson did the most extraordinary thing. He marched up to Holmes with his hands in front of him, cupping an object of some sort.

"Look here, sir," he said. "My wife found this in the crop of the goose."

Holmes took the object from Peterson and held it up to the light from the frosted window. It looked like a large diamond or ruby, except that it was the most beautiful blue in colour.

"And this was in the bird's crop, you say?" Holmes demanded.

"Yes, sir," Peterson said, slowly getting his breath back. "My wife was preparing the bird for the oven when she found it."

"In its crop?" I asked.

"That's the goose's throat, Dr. Watson," Peterson said.

"Yes, I know that," I said. "I meant, how on earth did it get there?"

"That, my dear Watson, is what we must find out," said Holmes. He let out a low whistle as he studied the gem in his hands. "By Jove, Peterson, do you know what this is?"

Peterson shrugged. "Not really, Mr. Holmes. But it looks valuable. Is it some sort of diamond?"

"No, not a diamond," said Holmes. "But in some ways this is far more valuable than a diamond. Peterson, I do believe you have recovered the missing *Blue Carbuncle*."

"You mean, the Countess of Morcar's blue carbuncle?" I stared at Holmes, then at Peterson, then back at the blue stone Holmes held in his hand. "The precious stone that was stolen from the Hotel Cosmopolitan just a few days ago?"

"The very same," said Holmes. "A plumber by the name of John Horner had been arrested, but the stone was never recovered. Until now."

I stared at the hat on the chair. "Then is our Mr. Baker somehow involved with the theft? I mean, if it is his hat, and it was his goose..."

Holmes rubbed his hands with glee. "That is what we must find out, my dear Watson. What a delightful little problem to present itself on this otherwise boring Christmas holiday."

The Blue Carbuncle 7.

HOLMES HANDED ME A pen and paper. "Be so kind, Watson, as to jot down this advertisement for Peterson to take along to put into the evening papers."

I wrote down the message as Holmes told me.

Found, one hat and one Christmas goose. Would Mr. Henry Baker kindly come to 221b Baker Street at 6.30 pm this evening to collect his lost belongings.

Holmes turned to Peterson, handing him the message and a five pound note. "Peterson, I want this to go out in all the evening papers."

"All of them, sir?" asked Peterson.

"All of them," said Holmes.

Peterson stared at the five pound note. "Even if I do them all, Mr. Holmes, sir, it won't come to this much."

"Ah," said Holmes. "But with the change I want

you to buy and bring back another goose, identical in size and weight to the one you and Mrs. Peterson will shortly be eating. I must have something to give Mr. Baker when he arrives."

With that, Peterson went off to do his errands, and Holmes carefully put the blue carbuncle in his safety deposit box.

"Well, Watson," he said. "Other than eating these fine scones of Mrs. Hudson's, there's not much else we can do until half past six, after which we might have a busy evening ahead of us, depending on what Mr. Henry Baker has to say."

Holmes added with a twinkle in his eye, "I suggest you spend the afternoon with your dear, loving wife, so she'll be sure to brush your hat before you come out again."

The Blue Carbuncle 8.

AS LUCK WOULD HAVE it I arrived back at 221b Baker Street at about 6.25pm, just as Mr. Baker himself arrived – I knew it was him because the poor man was wearing an ill-fitting beret – so I was able to let Mr. Baker in without disturbing Mrs. Hudson, and escort him up the stairs to where Sherlock Holmes was waiting.

On the way up the stairs I was able to confirm Mr. Baker was indeed overweight and didn't exercise much, for the strain of climbing the stairs had him breathing hard. I could also see beneath the beret that he had gray hair, cut short.

I wondered how much else of what Holmes had deduced from the hat would prove correct. But I could hardly ask the man if his wife still loved him. Or indeed if he had gas laid on at his house.

Besides, that was a trivial matter compared to the mystery of the blue carbuncle.

Holmes got straight to the point as we entered his

room. The hat was on the table, alongside a fresh, plump, snowy-white goose.

"Tell me, is this your hat, sir?" Holmes pointed to the hat.

Mr. Baker smiled. "It is indeed, Mr. Holmes, and I am most grateful for your finding it and keeping it for me. I've had to borrow this beret to come out this evening, and it really doesn't suit me."

"This hat was handed in two days ago," said Holmes. "I had expected to see an advertisement in the papers asking if anyone had found it."

Mr. Henry Baker managed a wan smile. "If only, Mr. Holmes, but I simply could not afford to. These last few years have been very difficult for me. I had already spent what little money I had on the goose, and then I foolishly had a few drinks to celebrate Christmas Eve. I simply did not have enough money to pay for an advertisement as well."

"I quite understand," said Holmes, with a knowing smile towards me.

"My wife was barely talking to me even before I lost the goose," Mr. Baker continued, "so you can imagine what a dreadful festive season we had, with nothing on the dinner table Christmas Day."

Another point to Holmes, I thought to myself.

"Ah, yes, about the goose," said Holmes. "I'm afraid it has been eaten."

Mr. Henry Baker looked from Holmes to the big, fat goose on the table, then back to Holmes. "Eaten? But then, what is this I am looking at? Is that not the goose?"

"That," said Holmes, "is *a* goose, but not *the* goose. It is a replacement goose," Holmes said. "You will recall your goose had a black bar across its tail feathers, and this one does not."

Mr. Baker stared at the goose on the table, obviously trying to remember the first goose. At length he shrugged his shoulders. "Did it?" he said. "I really took no notice."

Holmes smiled at Mr. Baker. "The first goose would not have stayed fresh this long, so we ate it and bought you this fresh goose to replace it. I hope this does not cause any problems for you?"

Mr. Henry Baker beamed back. "Problems? Not at all! I mean, a goose is a goose, is it not? And this one looks to be about the same size, only fresher."

Holmes handed the hat to Mr. Baker. "So, here is your hat, sir. I'm sorry that I allowed it to get a little dusty, but I'm sure Mrs. Baker will be able to clean it up for you."

Mr. Baker chuckled. "It has been a long time since Mrs. Baker worried about my hat, Mr. Holmes. "But at least I will see a smile on her face tonight when I arrive home with this fine bird."

"Then I suggest you take it away now and enjoy it as a late Christmas dinner tomorrow," said Holmes.

"You, sir, are most kind," said Mr. Baker, stuffing his beret into his pocket and putting his dusty bowler hat on his head. Then he slung the goose over his shoulder. As he reached the door he turned to us and said, "I do not know how I can thank you enough, Mr. Holmes."

"Well, there is one thing you might do for me," said Holmes. "I enjoyed the first goose very much. Would you kindly tell me where you bought it?"

"By all means," said Mr. Baker. "It came from the goose club at the Alpha Inn."

"The goose club?" I asked.

"We all pay a few pence each week over the year into a kitty which the landlord at the Alpha Inn keeps safe," Mr. Baker explained. "By the time Christmas comes around there is enough money for us to buy a nice Christmas goose each. So the landlord of the Alpha Inn gave me the goose, but where he got it from, I have no idea."

As Mr. Henry Baker opened the door to leave, I said, "Before you go, may I ask a personal question, Mr. Baker?"

"Go ahead," Mr. Baker said.

"I was just wondering if you had gas laid on in your home, that is all."

Mr. Baker stared at me in astonishment, then burst out laughing. "I cannot imagine why you would want to know such a thing, but the answer is no, sir. We get by with candles."

I closed the door as Mr. Baker left us, and turned to Holmes, ready to admit he had been right yet again.

The Blue Carbuncle 9.

"THAT SETTLES IT," SAID Holmes, rubbing his hands together gleefully.

"It does indeed," I said. "You were absolutely right, Holmes. Mr. Henry Baker has no gas in his house, poor fellow."

Holmes laughed. "My dear Watson, that was never in question. Except by you, of course. What *has* been settled is whether or not Mr. Baker was involved in the theft of the blue carbuncle."

I stared at Holmes. "It has?"

"Of course," said Holmes. "Clearly Mr. Baker was *not* involved, for if he knew the blue gem was in the goose he would have demanded the original bird he had lost. Instead he has left us, quite happily, with a replacement goose. Obviously Mr. Baker knows nothing whatsoever of the blue carbuncle being in his goose."

"So we have a mystery on our hands," I said. "Namely to find out who put the blue gem in the goose, because that person must be the thief."

"Exactly so," said Holmes.

"So what next?" I asked, certain that Holmes would already have formed a plan.

And of course, he had.

"Come, we must hurry to the Alpha Inn," said Holmes, grabbing his overcoat and bustling out of the door.

I quickly put on my hat and coat and rushed after Holmes into the dark, cold evening.

The Blue Carbuncle 10.

AFTER FIFTEEN MINUTES walking through the evening streets of London, and covered in a light dusting of snow, we found ourselves at the Alpha Inn.

It was early, so the bar was not crowded. Holmes ordered two beers from the landlord and immediately struck up a conversation.

"I have been hearing about your goose club, good sir," said Holmes. "Mr. Henry Baker speaks very highly of you. He showed me one of your geese, and I wondered if you might have any more available."

"Sorry," said the landlord as he pushed two tankards of frothy beer before us. "You've come to the wrong place."

"But this is the Alpha Inn, is it not?" Holmes asked.

The landlord laughed again. "It is, and we do have a goose club. But the geese don't come from here, you see. There's a man in Covent Garden who sells them to me."

"A Covent Garden goose dealer?" said Holmes, thinking quickly. "Why, you must surely mean Smith, perhaps? Or even Wilkinson?"

"Neither of those two, sir," said the landlord, pulling his watch from his pocket. "Breckinbridge is his name. He'll shortly be closing up for the night, though, so if you want to catch him this evening you'll have to hurry."

"In that case there is no time to lose," said Holmes. "Come, Watson."

And with that Holmes was dragging me out through the door.

"Steady on, Holmes!" I cried. "I didn't get to touch that beer!"

"No time for that now," said Holmes as he strode towards Covent Garden. "There is a mystery to be solved and that is far more important than eating and drinking."

"It might be to you, Holmes," I muttered as I hurried to catch up with my friend. "I was looking forward to that beer."

Holmes hailed a passing Hansom cab and told the driver to make haste to Covent Garden.

The two-wheeled carriage gave us a little shelter from the icy wind, but not much. I pitied the poor driver, sat out in the open, above us at the back, steering the horses.

Ten minutes later we arrived at London's famous market, by day the busiest marketplace in London, bustling with shoppers, but at this time of an evening all but deserted.

We were just in time to find Mr. Breckinbridge closing up his stall for the night.

"No geese, my man?" asked Holmes, rushing across. "I was told you had some fine specimens here on Christmas Eve."

"Sold out, guv'nor," said Mr. Breckinbridge. "Try my mate's stall at the end of the row. He still has a few left."

"But I wanted one of *your* geese," insisted Holmes, dismissing the other stall with a wave of his hand. "Your geese came highly recommended."

"Oh?" Mr. Breckinbridge, looking pleased with himself. "And who might be recommending my geese, may I ask?"

"Why, the landlord of the Alpha Inn," said Holmes. "He told me your geese were the best available by far, and I should go to no-one else but you. Absolutely no-one else will do, the landlord had said."

Mr. Breckinbridge swelled with pride. "Is that so? Well I did sell him a couple of dozen geese as it happens. But they've all gone. Sorry. Not a single goose left."

"Well, might I ask where you yourself got the geese from?" Holmes said.

Mr. Breckinbridge's smile disappeared. He stood with his arms crossed and glared at Holmes. "I don't see as that's any of your business, guv'nor."

Holmes shrugged. "It's a simple enough question, my man. Where did you buy the geese you sold to the landlord of the Alpha Inn? Is that too much to ask?"

Mr. Breckinbridge was having none of it. "Yes, sir, it *is* too much to ask. It's none of your business where I get my geese from, and you can't say otherwise."

Holmes turned to me, a sorrowful look on his face. "Then the bet's off, Watson. Sorry."

Mr. Breckinbridge stared at Holmes, then at me, then back at Holmes. "Bet, did you say?" Mr. Breckinbridge leaned forward. "What's all this about a bet?"

Holmes waved a hand at Mr. Breckinbridge. "No matter," he said. "It's just that I made a bet with my friend Watson here that the geese you sold were country bred, and he took on the bet, saying they were bred right here in the city."

Holmes of course had made no such bet with me. It was just a clever trick to make Mr. Breckinbridge reveal the information we needed. And it worked.

"Let me get this straight," said Mr. Breckinbridge, suddenly very interested. "You, sir, think them there geese were bred in the countryside, and your friend here thinks they was town-bred, is that right?"

"Exactly so," said Holmes. "I happen to be an expert on these things and I know a country-bred goose when I see one. It was quite obvious to me that those geese you sold the Alpha Inn were country-bred."

"And you and your fiend here have a fiver riding on this bet, right?" Mr. Breckinbridge said, leaning even closer.

"Precisely so, my good man," said Holmes. "Now if you will just tell my friend Watson here that those geese were indeed country-bred then I can claim my winnings and we can be on our way. Watson, bring that five pounds out of that moth-eaten wallet of yours. It's time to admit you were wrong and pay up. Isn't that right, Mr. Breckinbridge?"

"Hah! You lost your bet, mate," Mr. Breckinbridge said to Holmes with a smug smile. "Those birds is city bred, as sure as I am."

"Nonsense," said Holmes. "They were country-bred."

"Were not, so," said Breckinbridge. "Those geese were city-bred. Now pay the man. You've lost your bet fair and square."

"You're just saying that," said Holmes. "You can't prove those geese were city-bred, so it's just your word against mine."

"Oh, can't I?" said Mr. Breckinbridge. "It just so happens that I can prove it."

And with that Mr. Breckinbridge leaned beneath the stall and produced a thin book which he opened on the counter. We watched as he ran his finger down a list of sales and purchases.

"Now look you here, good sir," Mr. Breckinbridge said to Holmes, pointing to the list on the right hand page. What does that say?"

Holmes looked at where Mr. Breckinbridge's finger pointed, and read out loud the entry.

"Sold to the Alpha Inn. Twenty plump geese," Holmes read out. "And that is dated two days ago." He shrugged his shoulders. "So? That just shows that you sold them on to the Alpha Inn. It does not show where the geese came from in the first place."

Mr. Breckinbridge smiled smugly again, and ran his finger across the book to the left hand page.

"That's where the geese went," said Mr. Breckinbridge. "And here's where they came from, on the same line. Go on, guv'nor, read it out so your friend here knows the truth."

Holmes read it out. "Bought from Mrs. Margaret Oakshott, poultry supplier, 117 Brixton Road. Twenty plump home-bred geese, for re-sale to the Alpha Inn."

"And where is Brixton Road where them there geese was home-bred?" Mr. Breckinbridge was asking. "Is it in the city or in the country?"

"It's in the city, Holmes!" I exclaimed, joining in the play-acting. "By Jove! I was right! Those geese were town-bred, just as I said. You owe me five pounds!"

Mr. Breckinbridge looked as pleased as a lamb with two tails.

"There you go, Mr. So-Called Poultry Expert. You've lost your bet. Now pay the man. Right here in front of me. I'll be his witness." Mr. Breckinbridge put his hands on his hips and glared at Holmes.

"Come on, hand over that five pounds."

At this Holmes, pretending to be annoyed, thrust his hand into his pocket and pulled out a crisp five pound note which he handed to me. I took it solemnly and put it in my wallet.

"That will teach you, Holmes," I said, still play-acting. "You should have known better than to bet against a man with my knowledge of poultry."

"Bah!" said Holmes, and stormed off.

I tipped my hat to Mr. Breckinbridge and chased after my friend. As soon as we were out of sight we stopped and both laughed. I gave Holmes his five pound note back, of course.

It was too late by then to head off to Brixton Road where the geese had come from and it seemed solving the mystery of the blue carbuncle would have to wait until the morning.

But just as we prepared to head back to Baker Street we heard shouting over at the Breckinbridge stall, and suddenly the mystery was a whole lot nearer to being solved.

The Blue Carbuncle 11.

WE LOOKED BACK AT the Covent Garden market stalls and saw Mr. Breckinbridge arguing with a man who had arrived just as we left, and as both their voices were raised it was easy for us to hear what they said from our dark alley.

"What is it with you people today?" Mr. Breckinbridge was shouting. "Why is everybody suddenly interested in where it is I gets my geese from? In all my time selling birds here at Covent Garden no-one has ever asked before, and now suddenly two lots of people turn up wanting to know, one after the other. What, another bet, is it?"

"I don't know nothing about no other people and I don't know nothing about no bet," protested the man. "But one of them there geese was mine, and Mrs. Oakshott said she sent it to you by mistake."

"No mistake," said Mr. Breckinbridge. "I ordered and paid for those birds."

"But one of them was mine," the man repeated. "It

got mixed up with yours, that's all."

"Mrs. Oakshott has plenty more geese where those come from," said Mr. Breckinbridge. "Just ask her for another one."

"But this one was special," said the man.

"I bet it was," said Holmes quietly. "Watson, it looks like we have found our thief. Why else would anyone be so bothered about one particular goose? And no surprise at all that it is Ryder. He was my initial suspect."

I stared at Holmes. "You know him? And what do you mean, initial suspect? Holmes, we only knew that the blue carbuncle was in the goose's crop this afternoon."

My dear Watson," Holmes tutted. "The jewel was stolen several days ago, from the Hotel Cosmopolitan, as you well know. Obviously the official police have not asked for my help, so I could not investigate fully, but I took it upon myself to visit the hotel immediately the news broke, and I made some inquiries as to which staff might have had access to the Countess of Morcar's rooms. John Ryder and a maid he is friends with were both my prime suspects."

"You never fail to amaze me, Holmes," I said. "What do you propose we do now? I mean, we have no proof it was this fellow that was involved?"

"Not yet," said Holmes, "but we will soon enough. Come. When he leaves the market we will have a quiet word."

The Blue Carbuncle 12.

AND THAT'S WHAT happened. As soon as the man left Mr. Breckinbridge, Holmes and I walked quickly after him and caught up with him in another quiet alleyway just beyond Covent Garden.

Holmes stretched out a long arm and grabbed Ryder by the shoulder, wheeling the man around so his face was lit up by the light of the gas lamp.

"So, said Holmes firmly, "you are interested in one particular goose, are you? And why would that be, might I ask?"

"What business it is of yours?" The man glared defiantly at Holmes.

"What business is it of mine?" Holmes stared back hard at Ryder. "My name is Sherlock Holmes, and it is *my* business to know the business of people like *you*," Holmes said.

"You don't know nothing about me," said the man.

"On the contrary," said Holmes, "I know almost everything about you. You are trying t o find one particular goose. A goose which was bred at Mrs. Oakshott's poultry farm on Brixton Road and then sold to Breckinbridge at the Covent Garden market. The goose is white and has a black bar across its tail."

The man stared in amazement at Holmes. "That's the one! Do you know where it is?"

"I know exactly where it is," said Holmes. "Would you like me to take you there?"

"I most certainly would," said the man eagerly.

"First, I need some answers," said Holmes. "What is your name?"

The man hesitated, then said "John Richardson, that's who I am."

"No, this will not do," said Holmes. "Your real name, please, Mr. Ryder."

The man stared at Holmes, mouth open. "How on earth do you know that?"

Holmes turned to me. "Watson, as I said earlier, this is Mr. John Ryder, Head Attendant at the Hotel Cosmopolitan. The man who stole the blue carbuncle."

"It wasn't me!" shouted the man. "You've got it all wrong!"

"On the contrary," said Holmes. "I know almost everything that happened, but there is one small part I have not yet figured out, so we're going for a little ride, and then you will tell me everything."

Holmes kept a firm grip on John Ryder's shoulder with one hand and hailed a passing cab with the other. "221b Baker Street," he said.

John Ryder stared at Holmes. "What, you're not handing me over the police?"

"That remains to be seen," said Holmes. "We will discuss this further in the warmth of my rooms and I will make decision then as to what will happen to you. And I warn you now, Ryder, absolute honesty from you is your only hope of not going to prison."

The Blue Carbuncle 13.

HALF AN HOUR LATER we were back at Baker Street, where Mrs. Hudson had thoughtfully kept the fire blazing for us.

We settled down before the glowing coals and Holmes began talking. He had the safety box on his lap.

"I know most of what happened," Holmes said, "but I would like you to fill in the gaps where the picture is not so clear. And I warn you again, Ryder, be honest, for even one lie from you now and you will go to prison."

Ryder crossed his arms arrogantly. "For what? All you know is I am looking for a goose. That ain't no crime."

"But stealing something from the hotel where you work most certainly is a crime," said Holmes. "And letting someone else be blamed for it makes it all the worse."

"I don't know what you are talking about," said

the man.

"On the contrary," said Holmes, "you know exactly what I am talking about. This." Holmes opened the safety box to reveal the precious blue stone.

Ryder's mouth fell open. "How on earth?"

"When the news first broke of the missing blue carbuncle," said Holmes, "I took the liberty of visiting the hotel."

"I didn't see you there," said Ryder.

"That is because I did not want you to see me there," said Holmes. "But I was there, watching you. You and your accomplice, Catherine Cusack."

Ryder's eyes widened. "What about her?"

"Obviously you needed a helper who could easily enter and leave her ladyship's rooms," said Holmes, "and who better than Catherine Cusack, her ladyship's waiting-maid."

Ryder stared at the floor, saying nothing.

"So between the two of you you created some small problem a plumber would be needed to fix, and then called Mr. Horner, who you knew had been in trouble with the police in the past."

Ryder still said nothing.

"Mr. Horner did an honest job fixing the plumbing," said Holmes. "But then, when he had gone, you and Catherine Cusack stole the blue carbuncle and let Mr. Horner be arrested and put in prison, awaiting trial for a theft he knew nothing about."

At this Ryder lost control. The wretched man flung himself to the floor and grabbed Holmes by the leg.

"Please, Mr. Holmes," Ryder begged. "I am so sorry. Please don't call the police on me. I don't want to go to prison. I didn't mean no harm."

"You should have thought of that before, Ryder," Holmes said, pushing the man back to his chair. "There is an innocent man in jail right now, and it should be you and Cusack there in his place."

"Mr. Holmes, please, no!" screamed Ryder fearfully. "Let me go and I'll leave the country. That way the charges against Horner will be dropped because I won't be there to say anything against him."

"Hmmm," said Holmes. "I will think about that. But first I need you to tell me the one piece of this jigsaw I have not been able to work out."

"I will tell you anything you want to know," said Ryder. "Anything at all."

The Blue Carbuncle 14.

"ALL I WANT TO KNOW is this," said Holmes. "How did the blue carbuncle get into the crop of the goose? That is what mystifies me still."

Ryder took a deep breath and began his story.

"I knew the police might search me and my room at the hotel, Mr. Holmes, so I went out with the blue carbuncle in my pocket, pretending I had some business to attend," explained Ryder.

"And you went to Mrs. Oakshott's, the poultry-breeder on the Brixton road," said Holmes. "That much I can work out. But why go there at all, and how did the blue carbuncle get inside the goose's crop?"

"Mrs. Oakshott is my sister," said Ryder.

Holmes nodded. "It was my intention first thing tomorrow to find out if there was a connection between you, but your turning up at Coven Garden asking Breckinridge about the goose saved me a great deal of trouble."

Ryder said nothing.

"So come on, Ryder" urged Holmes. "Explain the last part of the mystery. I presume the goose did not try to eat the blue carbuncle by accident and then the stone got stuck in the goose's throat. So how did it get there?"

Ryder took a deep breath. "I had the blue carbuncle in my pocket, of course, and thought if I could just hide it somewhere for a few days I could come back and collect it later."

"But inside a goose?" I asked. "How on earth did you come up with that crazy idea?"

"I was out in the goose-yard, smoking my pipe, trying to think of where to hide the jewel, when the idea occurred to me," said Ryder. "Some weeks before, my sister had told me I could choose one of her geese and take it home for Christmas. I looked at all the geese running about and most of them looked identical, but there was one with a distinctive black bar across its tail so I grabbed it and forced the jewel down its throat."

"I would imagine that caused quite a commotion," I said. "Geese are not the quietest of creatures at the best of times."

Ryder was nodding his head. "The geese were so noisy my sister rushed out to see if a fox had somehow got into the yard. I let the goose go and they all rushed off to the far corner of the yard, making an enormous racket."

"So far this is all quite believable, Ryder," said

Holmes. "I think I can deduce the rest. Your sister told you to take your goose with you, so you grabbed a white goose with a black bar across its tail, killed it and took it home. But when you cut open the goose you found it was the wrong bird and that there had in fact been two birds with black bars across their tails. Is that what happened, Ryder?"

"It is, Mr. Holmes," said Ryder, looking sorry for himself. "It happened exactly like that."

"You went back to your sister's poultry farm, only to find you were too late and the other geese had been sold," Holmes said. "You asked who had bought them, and of course she told you it was Breckinbridge in Covent Garden. Then you came to Covent Garden to find Breckinbridge, which brings us full circle to where we are now."

"And that's the honest truth, Mr. Holmes," said Ryder. "So even though I did wrong and stole the jewel, I never gained anything by it." He stared at Holmes with pleading eyes. "Now what will happen to me?"

The Blue Carbuncle 15.

AT THIS HOLMES STRODE to the door, pulled it open, and pointed at Ryder. "Get out, Ryder, and never show your face in London ever again."

Ryder stared at Holmes. "Really, sir? Really?"

"Go now, before I change my mind," said Holmes sternly.

And with that John Ryder raced through the door and was never seen again.

The Blue Carbuncle 16.

MRS. HUDSON BROUGHT us up another pot of tea and more buttered scones with strawberry jam, and Holmes and I talked about the case further once Mrs. Hudson had gone.

The coal fire blazed in the grate, making us forget the cold outside.

"I imagine Ryder will be rushing off to his sister even as we sit here, to say his final farewells and make up some excuse as to why he is leaving," I said. "But what will happen to the plumber, John Horner?"

"The case against John Horner will be dropped, of course," said Holmes. "The police have no evidence he stole the jewel, because of course he is entirely innocent. And the only witness against him will never be seen around here again."

"But you let a criminal go," I said. "Two criminals, if we count Catherine Cusack. Ryder and Cusack both committed the crime. Surely they should be arrested and made to pay for their crimes?"

Holmes shrugged. "If the official police want to arrest him and take him to court that is their business, not mine. I am not paid to do their work for them."

"But…" I protested.

"But what?" Holmes asked. "The real culprits have not gotten away with their crime, Watson. No, this way they will not go to prison, it's true. But neither of them have the jewel, and they now both have no jobs, for I will go to the hotel tomorrow and tell the girl, Cusack, what I know. She will make her excuses and leave. They will never find work in London again."

"Yes," I said, "you are right, Holmes. That is probably the best way to end this matter. No-one has been harmed. Horner will soon be a free man. And two first-time thieves will have been frightened so much they will probably never even think about committing a crime again."

"Exactly so," said Holmes, biting into a buttered scone. "And after all, Watson, it is Christmas. The season for forgiveness."

The End

Thank you for reading.

Thank you for reading *Sherlock Holmes re-told for children : The Blue Carbuncle*, one of the *Classics For Kids : Sherlock Holmes* short story adaptations of the Sir Arthur Conan Doyle classics.

If you enjoyed it, please leave a review and tell your friends

There is a list at the end of this book of all titles currently available in *Classics For Kids : Sherlock Holmes* series. Plenty more to come!

Classics For Kids : Sherlock Holmes ebooks are available from all good ebook retailers worldwide and can be read on smartphones, tablets and e-readers.

Paperback and audio-book versions are also available.

There are lots more *Sherlock For Kids* titles on the way. To get updates on when new titles in this series are released, and for other new releases by this author, just email to

markwilliamsauthor@gmail.com

and ask to be put on the mailing list for *Classics For Kids : Sherlock Holmes* updates.

All author proceeds from the *Sherlock For Kids* series go towards supporting babies, children, families and schools in The Gambia, West Africa.

The
Classics For Kids : Sherlock Holmes
Series

The following titles are now available as ebooks from all good ebook retailers worldwide and may also be available as paperbacks and audio-books.

The Blue Carbuncle
Silver Blaze
The Red-Headed League
The Engineer's Thumb
The Speckled Band
The Six Napoleons
The Naval Treaty

Sherlock Holmes Re-told for Children
3-in-1
The Blue Carbuncle
Silver Blaze
The Red-Headed League

Sherlock Holmes Re-told for Children
3-in-1
The Engineer's Thumb
The Speckled Band
The Six Napoleons

Sherlock Holmes Re-told for Children
6-in-1
The Blue Carbuncle
Silver Blaze
The Red-Headed League
The Engineer's Thumb
The Speckled Band
The Six Napoleons

Coming next:

The Musgrave Ritual
The Beryl Coronet
The Gold Pince-Nez

33607788R00040

Made in the USA
Middletown, DE
16 January 2019